STOP STOP

STOP

by Edith Thacher Hurd

Pictures by CLEMENT HURD

HARPER & ROW, PUBLISHERS
New York, Evanston, and London

An I CAN READ Book

STOP STOP

STOP STOP

It was Saturday.

Suzie's mother and

Suzie's father had gone away.

They had gone away

for the whole day.

Funny old Miss Mugs

had come to stay with Suzie.

Suzie liked Miss Mugs, but

she thought she WASHED too much.

The first thing Miss Mugs said was,

"Suzie, get washed up, dear.

We are going to the zoo."

Then Miss Mugs began to wash.

First she washed

Suzie's hands and face.

9

Then she washed her neck.

She combed Suzie's hair

so hard it hurt.

"Ouch!" said Suzie.

"Stop! Stop!

Aren't we going to the zoo?"

11

Then Suzie had to change her dress.

Miss Mugs had found a spot.

Suzie wished Miss Mugs would let her

wear a nice dirty dress.

But Miss Mugs would not.

When Miss Mugs stopped

washing Suzie, she began

washing Suzie's house.

First she washed the dirty dishes.

Then she washed the dirty dog.

She put him in the bathtub.

She turned the water on.

"Oh dear, Miss Mugs,"

Suzie said.

"We never wash our dog."

"So I see," said old Miss Mugs.

The dog jumped out.

16

He ran away.

Suzie looked and looked.

Outside.

Inside.

Up the back stairs.

The dog was in the closet.

What a mess!

Miss Mugs had to wash all the clothes.

But she put in too much soap.

There were bubbles in the bathroom.

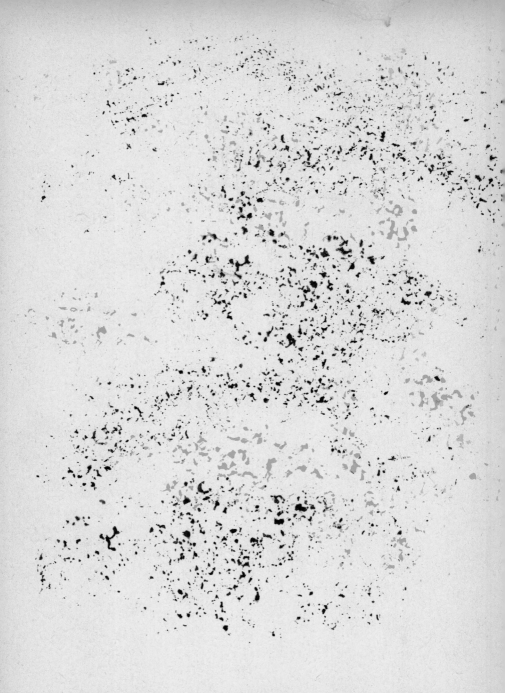

There were bubbles in the hall.

There were bubbles in the bird cage.

And that's not all.

"Oh, what trouble,"

Suzie said.

"Stop washing.

Please, Miss Mugs."

KERCHEW!

Suzie sneezed and sneezed.

"Our house is clean enough.

When ARE we going to the zoo?"

27

"Just let me mop the kitchen floor.

That dog made such a mess,"

said old Miss Mugs.

Then she mopped up everything.

28

She even mopped the cat.

Poor Miss Mugs.

The cat scratched back.

"Oh, I'm sorry," Suzie said.

"But our cat is very clean.

I never heard of mopping up a cat.

AREN'T we going soon?"

"I'll just do this rug,"

said old Miss Mugs.

31

"And my goodness!
Those curtains have some
dirty spots."

Miss Mugs got a ladder.

But it wasn't strong enough.

33

CRASH!

Down she went.

Down went Miss Mugs.

34

She bumped her head.

She hurt her toe.

"Oh, I'm sorry," Suzie said.

"But please stop.

You've washed enough.

Please, Miss Mugs.

Let's go."

So Miss Mugs stopped.

Then she said,

"Are you ready for the zoo?

Have you washed your face?

Have you combed your hair?

Are those clean socks?"

"Yes, yes, yes," Suzie said.

"Please, Miss Mugs.

Let's GO!"

First they passed a man

who was washing windows.

Miss Mugs said,

"You left some dirty spots."

Then they passed the garbage truck.

Miss Mugs said,

"How smelly!"

They passed the man

who cleans the street.

Miss Mugs said he wasn't neat.

The man got mad.

He waved his broom

and said,

"Look out!"

"Yes, please look out,

Miss Mugs,"

Suzie said.

"You may get into trouble.

You are making EVERYBODY mad."

But Miss Mugs did not look out.

At the zoo she said,

"These monkeys are not clean."

43

The monkeys laughed at her.

Then she said,

"That bear's fur should be white."

45

He growled at her.

"This hippopotamus has not
brushed his teeth just right."

He sneezed at her.

"This gorilla's finger nails

are BLACK."

She turned her back.

"This lion has not combed his mane."

51

He roared at her.

"I would like

to wash that neck,"

said old Miss Mugs.

"And scrub those spots."

Then Miss Mugs and Suzie

watched the elephants.

They watched the mother elephant
give her baby elephant a bath.
"That baby looks so nice and clean,"
Miss Mugs said.
"But she forgot his ears."

The mother elephant looked at

old Miss Mugs.

57

Then she lifted her long trunk

AND———————

gave MISS MUGS a bath!

"Stop! Stop!" said old Miss Mugs.

But the elephant did not stop.

At last the keeper shouted:

"ELEPHANT, ELEPHANT!
TURN THE WATER OFF!"

So the elephant turned

the water off.

Miss Mugs was a mess.

"Oh dear," Suzie said.

"Now you will have to go right home.

You have to wash your hands and face.

You have to change your dirty dress."

"Not I," said old Miss Mugs.

"I've washed and scrubbed

and soaped all day.

I've had enough of that.

Who cares about my hands and face?

Who cares about my dirty dress?

Let's have a little fun."

And so they did.

Suzie on a lion,

Miss Mugs on a goat.